To MJF

tiger tales
an imprint of ME Media, LLC
202 Old Ridgefield Road, Wilton, CT 06897
Published in the United States 2006
Originally published in Great Britain 2005
By Little Tiger Press
An imprint of Magi Publications
Text and illustrations ©2005 Kanako Usui
CIP data is available
ISBN 1-58925-054-0
Printed in China
1 3 5 7 9 10 8 6 4 2

# The Fantastic Mr. Wani

## by Kanako Usui

Mr. Wani

Hello, Mr. Wani! We are having a party at 11 o'clock on Sunday. Please come and join us!

The Froggies

Mr. Wani, the crocodile, was in a hurry.
He was almost late for a party in town.
So he began to run.

He ran and ran, faster and faster...

but his little legs couldn't keep up!

# Oops!

He tripped,
tumbled,
and bounced....

**Meanwhile, a little way down the road,
four mice were also on their way to a party.**

"I'm sorry I squashed you," said Mr. Wani. "I'm rushing to a party, and I'm afraid I'll be late. I just don't know what to do!"

The mice were very kind, and they put their heads together for him.

"I have an idea!" cried Miss Mouse.
"Let's use these

# balloons!

You can fly to the party!"

Town ⇨

The mice tied the balloons to Mr. Wani's mouth.
"You're a genius, Miss Mouse!" said Mr. Wani.
"If I fly, I'll definitely get to the party on time!"
Mr. Wani ran and ...

took off!

Up in the sky, Mrs. Crow was rushing to a party when she came across what she thought were lots of colorful floating lollipops.

# "Ooh! Delicious!"

she said, and she swooped
down to gobble them up!

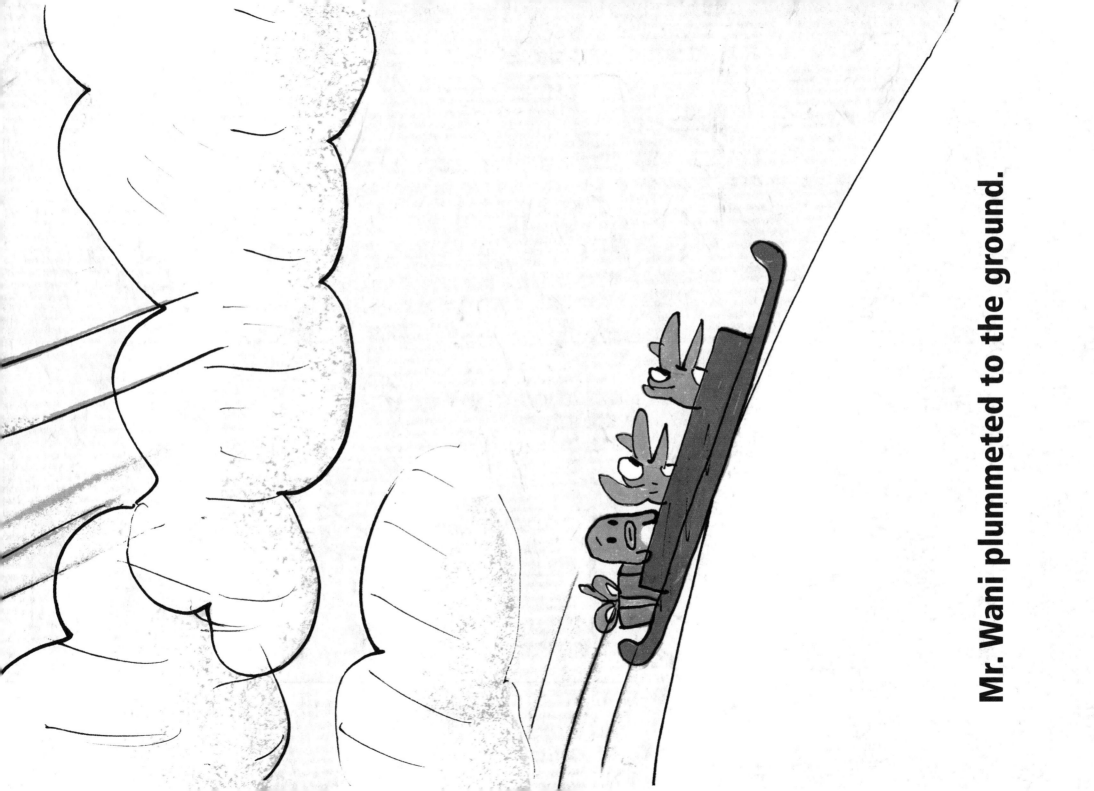

Mr. Wani plummeted to the ground.

# Crash!

Mr. Wani landed right on top of three penguins!

The penguins were very upset because Mr. Wani had broken their sled.

"Oh no! What can we do? How will we get to the party?" cried the penguins.

Mr. Wani felt sorry for them. So he offered to take them down the hill.

**But the Mr. Wani sled went**
faster **and faster and faster!**
**Finally it flew out of control and the penguins were thrown high into the sky.**

**Mr. Wani sped on . . .**

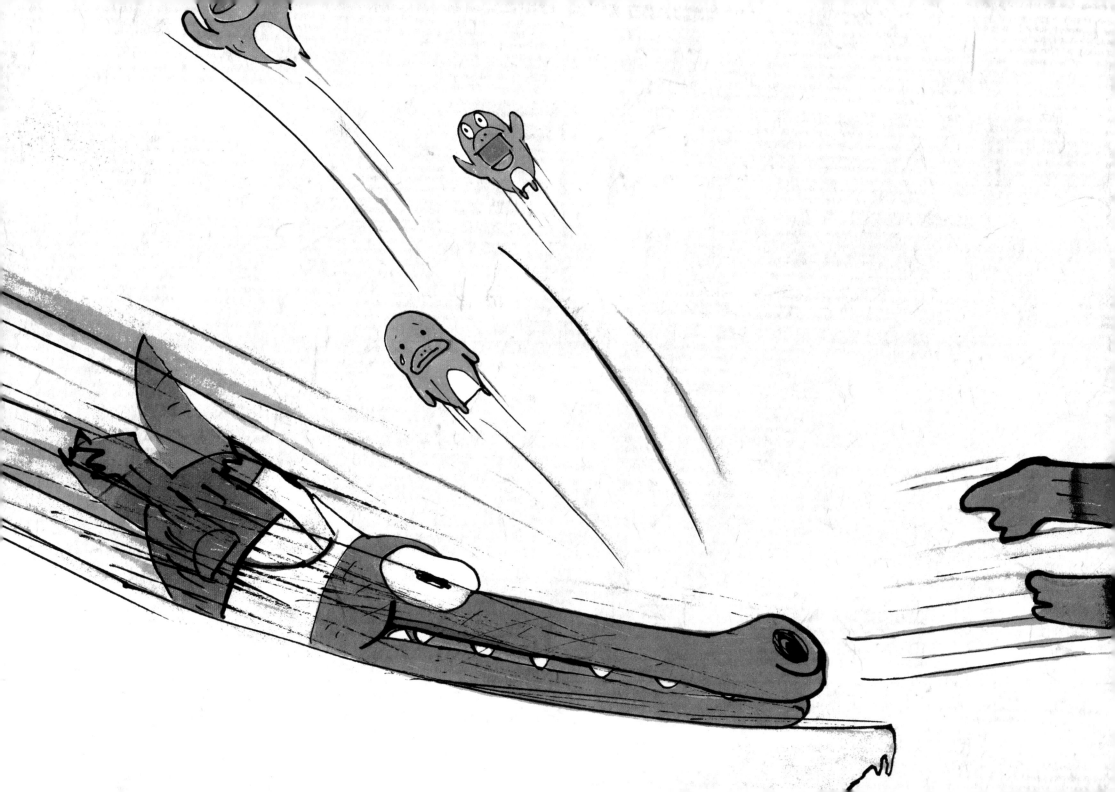

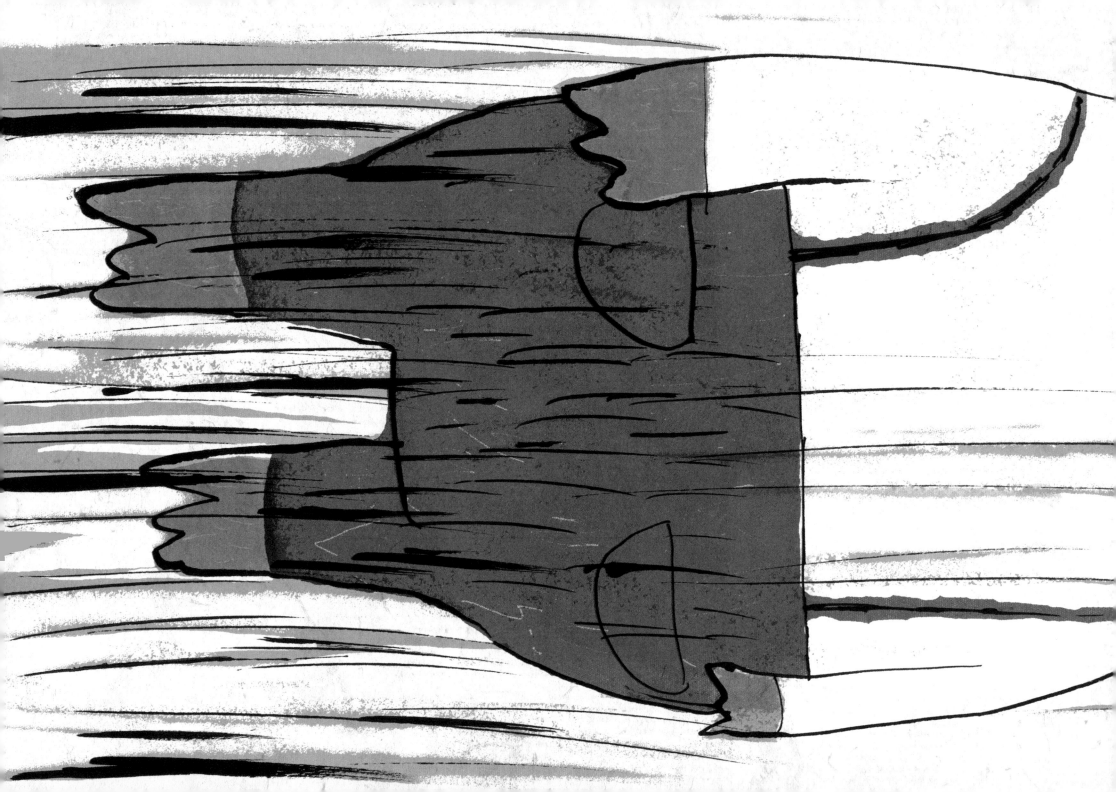

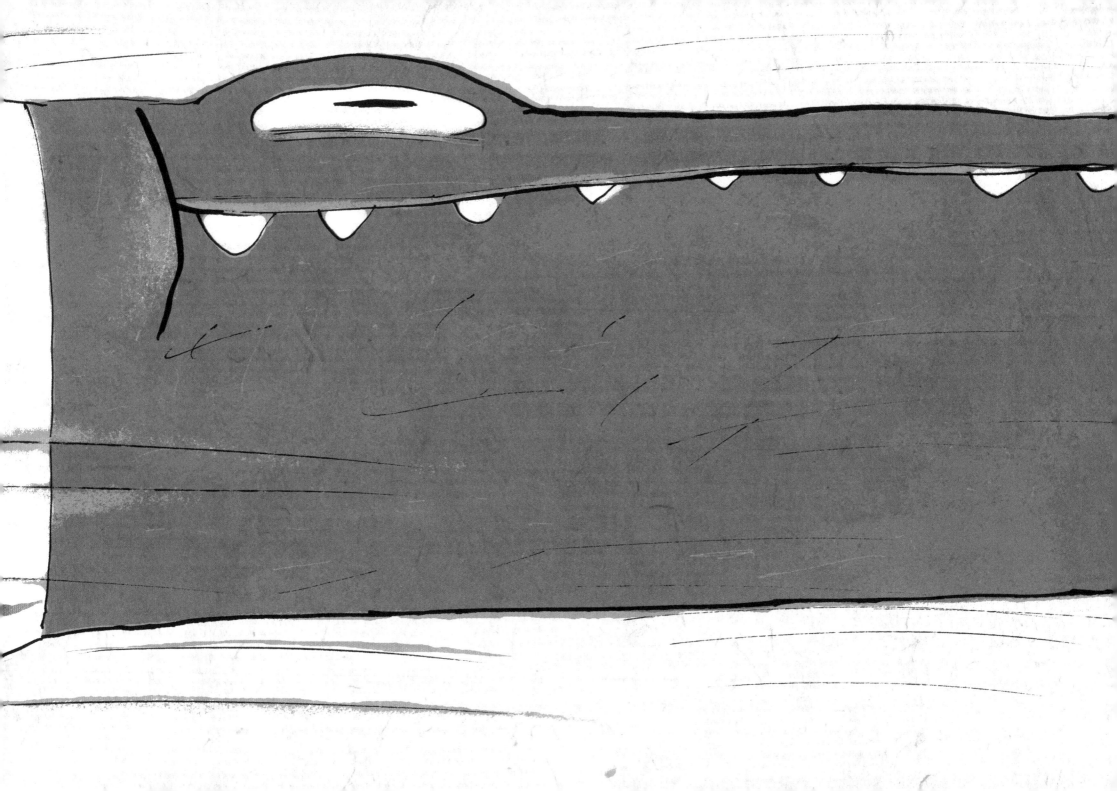

# Bump! into Mr. Elephant.

# Screech!

**Mr. Elephant skidded to a stop.**

Mr. Wani was flung into the air and landed right on top of a prickly hedgehog!

Mr. Wani bounced and bounced, higher and higher. **"Yikes!"** he cried...

Froggies

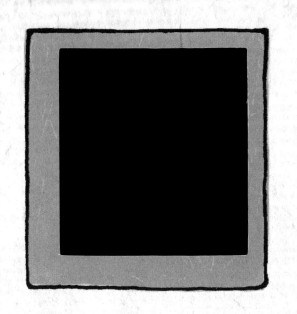

and landed right in the middle of the party!

"Hi, Mr. Wani! Have a chip," said the Froggies.

Mr. Wani's new friends were there, too.

The party went on for the whole day, and they all had a

# wonderful time.

In the evening, after everyone had left,
Mr. Tortoise showed up.
He was very, very late. . . .